HOLT, RINEHART AND WINSTON, INC.

COPYRIGHT © 1970 BY HOLT, RINEHART AND WINSTON, INC.
PUBLISHED SIMULTANEOUSLY IN CANADA
PRINTED IN THE UNITED STATES OF AMERICA
LIBRARY OF CONGRESS NUMBER 73-109195
STANDARD BOOK NUMBER 03-0845830-7

NEW YORK, TORONTO, LONDON, SYDNEY

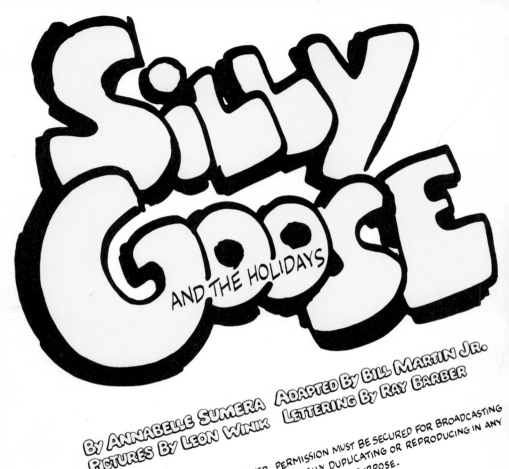

SILLY GOOSE

AND THE HOLIDAYS

By Annabelle Sumera   Adapted By Bill Martin Jr.
Pictures By Leon Winik   Lettering By Ray Barber

The Bill Martin Instant Reader